DAISY

Based on *The Railway Series* by the Rev. W. Awdry

Illustrations by
Robin Davies and Jerry Smith

EGMONT

EGMONT

We bring stories to life

First published in Great Britain in 2005
by Egmont UK Limited
239 Kensington High Street, London W8 6SA
This edition published in 2008
All Rights Reserved

Thomas the Tank Engine & Friends™

CREATED BY BRITT ALLCROFT

Based on the Railway Series by the Reverend W Awdry
© 2008 Gullane (Thomas) LLC. A HIT Entertainment company.
Thomas the Tank Engine & Friends and Thomas & Friends are trademarks of Gullane (Thomas) Limited.
Thomas the Tank Engine & Friends and Design is Reg. U.S. Pat. & Tm. Off.

HiT entertainment

ISBN 978 1 4052 3476 4
1 3 5 7 9 10 8 6 4 2
Printed in Italy

The Forest Stewardship Council (FSC) is an international, non-governmental organisation
dedicated to promoting responsible management of the world's forests. FSC operates a
system of forest certification and product labelling that allows consumers to identify
wood and wood-based products from well managed forests.

For more information about Egmont's paper buying policy please visit www.egmont.co.uk/ethicalpublishing

For more information about the FSC please visit their website at www.fsc.uk.org

TO THE TRAINS ➡

This is a story about Daisy the Diesel Rail-car. She worked at my station while Thomas was being repaired. She was bossy and thought she always knew best, but she soon learnt not to be so bullish …

One day, when Thomas was being repaired, The Fat Controller brought Daisy to work at the station.

"Look at me!" she said to the passengers. "I'm highly sprung and right up to date. After travelling with me, you won't want to ride in Thomas' bumpy carriages again!"

The passengers climbed aboard and waited for Daisy to set off.

Every morning, milk was collected from the farms and put on a wagon at the station. The wagon was coupled to Thomas' first train of the day, so he could take it to the Dairy. That day, the milk wagon was waiting for Daisy.

"I won't take that!" she said, in horror.

"Nonsense," said her Driver. "Come on now, it won't take long."

But Daisy refused to move.

Daisy lied so she wouldn't have to take the wagon.

"My Fitter says I'm highly sprung and pulling is bad for my swerves," she said.

"I can't understand it," said a workman. "Whatever made The Fat Controller send us such a feeble –"

"F-f-f-feeble!" spluttered Daisy, crossly.

"Stop arguing!" cried the passengers. "We're already late."

Nothing Daisy's Driver or Guard said would change her mind, so workmen moved the milk wagon and Daisy went smugly away.

"I made up a clever story," she chuckled to herself. "Now I can do the jobs I want to do and no more!"

When Toby came to the station, he was surprised to see the milk wagon there.

"Daisy's left the milk," Percy said, crossly. "Now I'll have to make a special journey with it and I'm already late for the Quarry."

"Why don't I take the milk to the Dairy and you fetch my Quarry trucks?" Toby said. "That way we can both save time."

It was agreed and both engines set off.

A little later, Toby met Daisy at a Junction. She laughed at his side-plates and cow-catchers. Toby explained that he had them to stop animals being hurt if they got on to the track in front of him.

"You're just scared!" Daisy said, rudely. "If I see an animal on the track, I'll toot and it will move!"

"I'm not scared," Toby replied, calmly. "And they won't just move if you toot!"

"They will for me," said Daisy, proudly.

When Daisy reached the next station, a policeman waved for her to stop.

"Champion, the bull, is on the track," he said. "Please move him along to the farmer."

"I'll show Toby how to manage animals," Daisy said to her Driver.

But she was about to be surprised …

"Move on!" tooted Daisy when she saw the bull, but Champion didn't move.

After a while, he became curious and slowly walked towards Daisy.

"Ooh!" said Daisy, nervously. "Look at his big horns. If I bump into them, he might hurt – er – himself."

She quickly backed away and left.

Meanwhile, Percy had picked up Toby's trucks. He was still grumpy about Daisy, so he was rude to the trucks. The trucks decided to teach him a lesson.

When he pulled them over a big hill, they shoved him forward, sending him racing out of control.

"Help!" Percy cried as he flew through a level crossing and crashed into some stone trucks in the yard.

Toby was leaving the station when Daisy crept back. One of her passengers told him what had happened.

"Now you know why my side-plates and cow-catchers are so useful!" Toby chuckled.

Just then, a workman told them about Percy's crash.

"If you help Percy," Toby said to Daisy, "I'll take your passengers and move the bull."

Daisy agreed and both engines set off.

Daisy worked hard all afternoon. She moved all the stone trucks away from the track, so the breakdown train could rescue Percy.

The Fat Controller came to speak to Daisy. "I heard that you left the milk wagon," he said, crossly. "I won't have lazy engines working on my Railway! However, you have done a good job here so, if you promise to work hard and listen to the other engines, you can stay on."

"Thank you, Sir," said Daisy, humbly.

Thomas came back to work the next day. Daisy stayed on to help while Percy was being repaired. The Fat Controller was very pleased because she had worked hard and listened to the other engines.

Daisy became good friends with the engines and, sometimes, she even delivered the milk wagon for Thomas!

The Thomas Story Library is THE definitive collection of stories about Thomas and ALL his friends.

5 more Thomas Story Library titles will be chuffing into your local bookshop in August 2008!

Jeremy
Hector
BoCo
Billy
Whiff

And there are even more Thomas Story Library books to follow later
So go on, start your Thomas Story Library NOW!

A Fantastic Offer for Thomas the Tank Engine Fans!

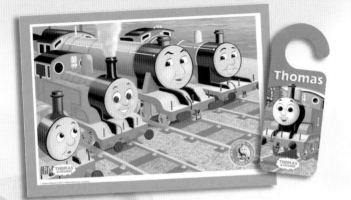

STICK
POUND
COIN
HERE

In every Thomas Story Library book like this one, you will find a special token. Collect 6 Thomas tokens and we will send you a brilliant Thomas poster, and a double-sided bedroom door hanger! Simply tape a £1 coin in the space above, and fill out the form overleaf.

TO BE COMPLETED BY AN ADULT

To apply for this great offer, ask an adult to complete the coupon below and send it with a pound coin and 6 tokens, to:
THOMAS OFFERS, PO BOX 715, HORSHAM RH12 5WG

☐ Please send a Thomas poster and door hanger. I enclose 6 tokens plus a £1 coin. (Price includes P&P)

Fan's name..

Address..

....Postcode...........................

Date of birth...

Name of parent/guardian...

Signature of parent/guardian...

Please allow 28 days for delivery. Offer is only available while stocks last. We reserve the right to change the terms of this offer at any time and we offer a 14 day money back guarantee. This does not affect your statutory rights.

☐ Data Protection Act: If you do not wish to receive other similar offers from us or companies we recommend, please tick this box. Offers apply to UK only.

Cut along the dotted line